# JUST BEYOND™

## WELCOME TO BEAST ISLAND

Published

More Books in the

# JUST BEYOND™

Graphic Novel Series

THE SCARE SCHOOL

THE HORROR AT HAPPY LANDINGS

WELCOME TO BEAST ISLAND

MONSTROSITY

# JUST BEYOND™

## WELCOME TO BEAST ISLAND

Written by
**R.L. Stine**

Illustrated by
**Kelly & Nichole Matthews**

Lettered by
**Mike Fiorentino**

Cover by
**Julian Totino Tedesco**

*Just Beyond* created by
**R.L. Stine**

Designer
**Scott Newman**

Associate Editor
**Sophie Philips-Roberts**

Editor
**Bryce Carlson**

BOOM! Studios, 5670 Wilshire Boulevard, Suite 400, Los Angeles, CA 90036-5679. Printed in USA. First Printing.

ISBN: 978-1-68415-612-2, eISBN: 978-1-64668-024-5

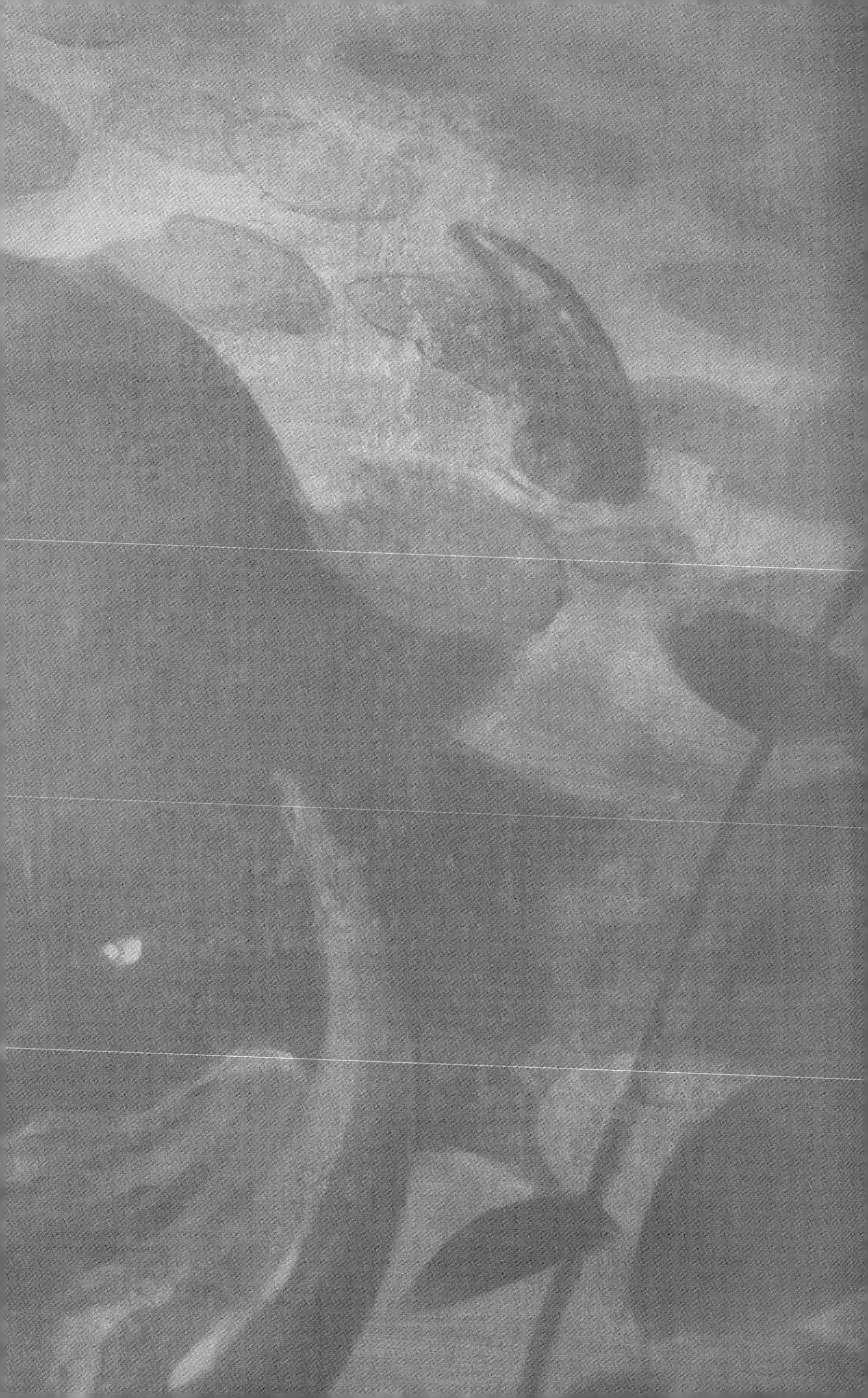

CHAPTER ONE
WHAT DOES MALA SUERTE MEAN?
THE OCEAN WAS ROUGH, AND UNCLE BILL'S BOAT WAS SMALL. I FELT LIKE I WAS RIDING ONE OF THOSE BUCKING RODEO BULLS...
BUT MY BROTHER BENNY AND I WERE EXCITED TO GO ON A SCIENTIFIC TRIP WITH UNCLE BILL. EXCITED... AND FRIGHTENED.
UNCLE BILL EXPLORES THE WORLD, FINDING NEW SPECIES OF ANIMALS. HE WAS TAKING US ON OUR FIRST TRIP--TO AN ISLAND IN THE MIDDLE OF NOWHERE.
I'M KARLA WILLIAMS. I'M 13 AND MY BROTHER BENNY IS 10. WE HAD A MILLION QUESTIONS FOR UNCLE BILL.

WHERE IS *MALA SUERTE* ISLAND?
I'M POINTING TO IT.
YOU'RE JUST POINTING TO THE PACIFIC OCEAN.
*MALA SUERTE* IS TOO SMALL TO SHOW UP ON ANY MAP.
AND IF I CAN FIND ANIMAL SPECIES THERE THAT NO ONE HAS EVER SEEN BEFORE, I'LL BE ***FAMOUS.***
IF YOU DISCOVER A NEW ANIMAL, WILL YOU NAME IT AFTER ME?
HAHA. FOR SURE. THE BENNY. PROBA-BLY SOME KIND OF TOAD.
*CROAK. CROAK.* I'M A BENNY. *CROAK. CROAK.* I LIKE TO EAT FLIES.

MAYBE I'LL BE A NEW BREED OF PANTHER. OR AN AWESOME CHEETAH!
NO. NO WAY. THERE ARE NO DANGEROUS ANIMALS LIKE THAT. IT'S A TINY ISLAND, MOSTLY A SWAMP.

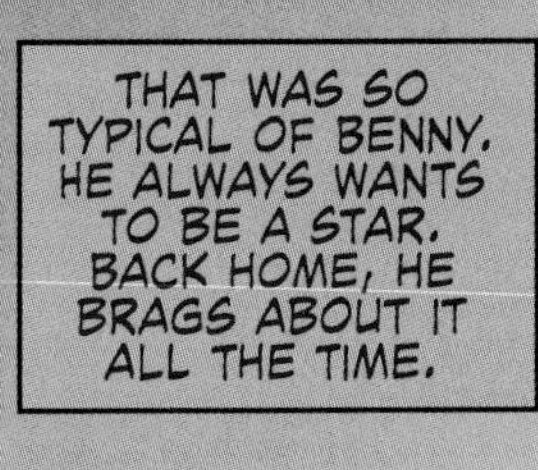
THAT WAS SO TYPICAL OF BENNY. HE ALWAYS WANTS TO BE A STAR. BACK HOME, HE BRAGS ABOUT IT ALL THE TIME.

I COULD BE A ROCK STAR. OR MAYBE I'LL BE A YOUTUBE STAR. THEY MAKE A TON OF MONEY, DON'T THEY?

WHY CAN'T YOU JUST BE YOU? WHAT MAKES YOU THINK YOU'LL BE A STAR?
I JUST HAVE A HUNCH. I FEEL LIKE I COULD BE A STAR!

THE ISLAND IS A SWAMP? YOU NEVER TOLD US.
I HAVE ANOTHER CONFESSION TO MAKE...

I KNEW YOUR PARENTS WOULD SAY NO. SO, I TOLD THEM WE WERE GOING TO DISNEY WORLD.

YOU MEAN...THEY DON'T KNOW WHERE WE ARE?

IT WAS A CRAZY THING TO DO. BUT I REALLY WANTED YOU TO COME ALONG.
AND IT'S TOTALLY SAFE?

SOME SCIENTISTS WARNED ME NOT TO GO. BUT THEY WERE JUST TRYING TO HOLD ME BACK. WE'LL BE FINE, WHAT CAN HAPPEN ON A TINY ISLAND?

...
WHAT DOES *MALA SUERTE* MEAN, UNCLE BILL?

NEVER MIND.
NO. SERIOUSLY. TELL US. WHAT DOES *MALA SUERTE* MEAN?

WELL...UH...IT MEANS "BAD LUCK." BUT...IT'S JUST A NAME. YOU'RE NOT SUPERSTITIOUS-- ***ARE*** YOU?

WE STEPPED ONTO THE DOCK. IT SEEMED THE WHOLE ISLAND HAD COME OUT TO GREET US. WHAT A WELCOME!
CAN I HELP YOU WITH YOUR BAGS, SIR?
HOW WAS YOUR JOURNEY? DO YOU NEED A PLACE TO STAY?
PLEASE-- SAMPLE THIS FRESH COCONUT MILK.

WOW. I DIDN'T KNOW MILK CAME FROM COCONUTS!
UNCLE BILL, THEY SEEM SO GLAD TO SEE US.
THEY DON'T GET MANY VISITORS.
WELCOME. ALL VISITORS TO *MALA SUERTE* MUST BEGIN AT SACRED HOUSE. THERE YOU WILL LEARN OF OUR HISTORY.

I READ ABOUT SACRED HOUSE. ALL OF THE TREASURES OF THE ISLAND ARE STORED HERE. LOOK AT THAT ANCIENT JADE MASK.
BENNY HAD HIS EYES ON THE MASK AND DIDN'T SEE THE ANIMAL SCULPTURE ON THE FLOOR.
OOOPS.
BENNY!
THAT THING TRIPPED ME!
DO YOU THINK YOU'LL EVER OUTGROW BEING A KLUTZ?
DO YOU THINK YOU'LL EVER OUT-GROW BEING YOU?!
DON'T FIGHT. REMEMBER? THIS IS A SACRED PLACE. HELP YOUR BROTHER UP, KARLA.

LET GO OF ME! I DON'T NEED YOUR HELP.
BENNY JERKED AWAY FROM ME. HE LURCHED TO HIS FEET--AND STUMBLED INTO A DISPLAY...
UH OH.
...I GASPED AS HE SENT THE ANCIENT JADE MASK CRASHING TO THE FLOOR.
OH NO!!
SMAAAAASH
IT'S AN ANCIENT DEATH MASK. BENNY--YOU DESTROYED IT!

IT WASN'T MY FAULT. KARLA PUSHED ME!
YOU LIAR! I DIDN'T TOUCH YOU!
WHILE BENNY AND I ARGUED, WE DIDN'T SEE THE WOMAN WHO STEPPED OUT OF THE SHADOWS.
UH...HELLO. WE'VE HAD AN ACCIDENT.
IT WAS NO ACCIDENT. IT WAS AN OMEN.
YOU SHATTERED YOUR GOOD LUCK WHEN YOU BROKE THE HOLY DEATH MASK. LEAVE THE ISLAND NOW.
BUT-- BUT--
I SAY THIS AS A FRIEND. HEED MY WORDS. IF YOU DON'T LEAVE NOW...YOU WILL NEVER SURVIVE KOROKO!

CHAPTER TWO
WHERE DID BENNY GO?
WHAT DID THAT STRANGE WOMAN MEAN, UNCLE BILL? WHAT IS KOROKO?
BEATS ME. I'VE NEVER HEARD THAT WORD BEFORE, IT MUST BE LOCAL SLANG. PERHAPS MARISSA KNOWS IT.
IS DR. NEWTON ALREADY HERE?
MARISSA NEWTON IS UNCLE BILL'S LAB PARTNER. HE SAID SHE WAS VERY SMART AND VERY NICE. I WAS EAGER TO MEET HER.
YES. SHE ARRIVED LAST WEEK TO SET THINGS UP FOR OUR ANIMAL STUDIES.
WELCOME·INN
HERE'S WHERE WE ARE STAYING. WE'LL DROP OUR BAGS AND GO FIND SOME LUNCH.
YAY, LUNCH. MY FAVORITE WORD!
HA. WE ALL KNOW YOUR FAVORITE WORD IS "BENNY"!
HELLO, SIR. WELCOME TO WELCOME INN. HOW CAN I HELP YOU?
WELC
WE HAVE RESERVED TWO ROOMS. THE NAME IS DR. BILL HARLAN.
HARLAN. LET ME LOOK.
COME
HARLAN... HARLAN... HMM. I'M NOT FINDING IT, SIR.

I'M SURE MY ASSISTANT MADE THE RESERVATION. PLEASE KEEP CHECKING.
SO SORRY. I DON'T HAVE IT. AND I'M AFRAID THE INN IS COMPLETELY FULL.
WELC
THAT'S IMPOSSIBLE. YOU HAVE NO ROOMS AT ALL?
NOT EVEN A BROOM CLOSET. SO SORRY, SIR.
WE HAVE NO PLACE TO STAY? WHERE WILL WE SLEEP?
DON'T PANIC, BENNY. LET ME HANDLE THIS.
YOU BROUGHT US BAD LUCK, BENNY. YOU BROKE THAT JADE MASK.
SHUT UP. ALL OF A SUDDEN YOU'RE SUPER-STITIOUS?
CAN I SPEAK TO DR. MARISSA NEWTON? IS SHE IN HER ROOM?
I'LL LOOK IT UP FOR YOU, SIR.
I HAVE A RESERVATION HERE FOR DR. NEWTON. BUT SHE NEVER ARRIVED.

THAT'S IMPOSSIBLE! SHE *HAS* TO BE HERE. LET ME CALL HER.
I'M SO SORRY, SIR. THERE'S NO PHONE SERVICE ON THE ISLAND. NO PHONES AT ALL.
ME
BUT... MARISSA *HAD* TO ARRIVE. IT'S BEEN A WEEK. TELL ME, SIR, IS THERE ANOTHER INN ON THE ISLAND? SOMEWHERE WE CAN STAY?
HE'S GONE. WOW.
HE WASN'T EXACTLY HELPFUL.
WE'LL FIND SOMEWHERE ELSE TO STAY. I'M NOT WORRIED. IT'S A VERY FRIENDLY ISLAND.
EXCEPT FOR THAT HOTEL CLERK.

I'M WORRIED ABOUT MARISSA. WHAT COULD HAVE HAPPENED TO HER?
UNCLE BILL, DO YOU THINK THERE'S ANOTHER INN HERE?
IF WE CAN'T FIND ANOTHER INN, I'M SURE SOME NICE PERSON WILL PUT US UP.
WE STARTED TO CROSS THE DIRT STREET. BUT A WOMAN BLOCKED OUR PATH. SHE PUSHED A STRANGE DOLL IN OUR FACES.
KOROKO! KOROKO! GET AWAY WHILE YOU CAN!

WEIRD. WHAT *IS* THAT CREATURE?
KOROKO! PLEASE--I BEG YOU!
NO. NO THANK YOU. NO DOLL FOR US.
THAT UGLY DOLL GAVE ME A SHIVER. SHE WAS THE SECOND ISLAND WOMAN TO SAY THE NAME KOROKO!
I THINK THAT'S A CAFÉ. WE CAN GET SOME LUNCH.

BENNY, IT'LL BE YOUR FIRST ISLAND FOOD.
BENNY? HEY--BENNY? WHERE *IS* HE?
HE WAS GONE. MY BROTHER HAD VANISHED INTO THIN AIR!

CHAPTER THREE
KOROKO? WHAT IS KOROKO?
UNCLE BILL AND I STOOD THERE IN TOTAL PANIC. THEN WE HEARD BENNY'S SHOUT.
BENNY!
HELLLP! HELLLP ME!
WE WENT RUNNING TOWARD HIS VOICE. I GOT THERE FIRST. BENNY HAD FALLEN INTO A DEEP SAND HOLE.
HELP! GET ME OUT OF HERE!
A MAN CAME RUNNING OVER AND HELPED UNCLE BILL AND ME PULL BENNY FROM THE HOLE.
READY? WE'LL ALL PULL TOGETHER.
BENNY SUDDENLY WEIGHED TWO TONS. BUT WE PULLED HIM OUT OF THE HOLE AND BRUSHED HIM OFF.
IT'S QUICKSAND! IT WAS PULLING ME DOWN.
THERE'S NO QUICKSAND ON THIS ISLAND, BENNY.
BUT MANY SAND HOLES TO WATCH OUT FOR. YOU WERE LUCKY IT WASN'T DEEPER.

MY NAME IS RAMAR BERNARD. LET ME TREAT YOU TO LUNCH AT THE CAFÉ.
THINK YOU CAN MAKE IT ACROSS THE STREET WITHOUT FALLING IN A HOLE?
THINK YOU CAN MAKE IT ACROSS THE STREET WITHOUT BEING A JERK?
THIS IS GOOD. WHAT IS IT?
IT'S MONKEY BRAINS. MONKEY BRAIN BURGERS ARE AN ISLAND SPECIALTY HERE.
ULLLP.
OH, WOW. IS THERE KETCHUP I COULD PUT ON IT?
I SEE YOU ARE ENJOYING THE ROASTED WATER BUGS. THEY MELT IN YOUR MOUTH, DON'T THEY?
ULLP. I THOUGHT THEY WERE RAISINS.
YOU STILL HAVE YOUR SUITCASES. WAS THERE NO ROOM AT WELCOME INN?
NO. I'M AFRAID THEY LOST OUR RESERVATION.

MY HOUSE IS BIG. YOU MUST COME STAY WITH ME.
BUT--
PLEASE. I INSIST. I WILL SHOW YOU ISLAND HOSPITALITY.
WELCOME. YEARS AGO, MY ANCESTORS BUILT A SMALL BAMBOO HUT ON THIS ISLAND. *MALA SUERTE* HAS BEEN GOOD TO ME. I BUILT THIS HOUSE WITH EVERY LUXURY.

WOW. WHAT'S THIS?
IT'S A BLOWGUN. IT'S USED TO SHOOT POISON DARTS.
HAVE YOU USED IT?
HAHA. I'D RATHER NOT SAY.
MY CRAZY BROTHER DECIDED TO TRY IT.
FWOOOOSH
LOOK OUT!
THUNNNNK
OOPS. I DIDN'T KNOW THERE WAS A DART INSIDE IT! SORRY!
NO HARM DONE. BUT YOU MUST TAKE CARE HERE, YOUNG MAN.

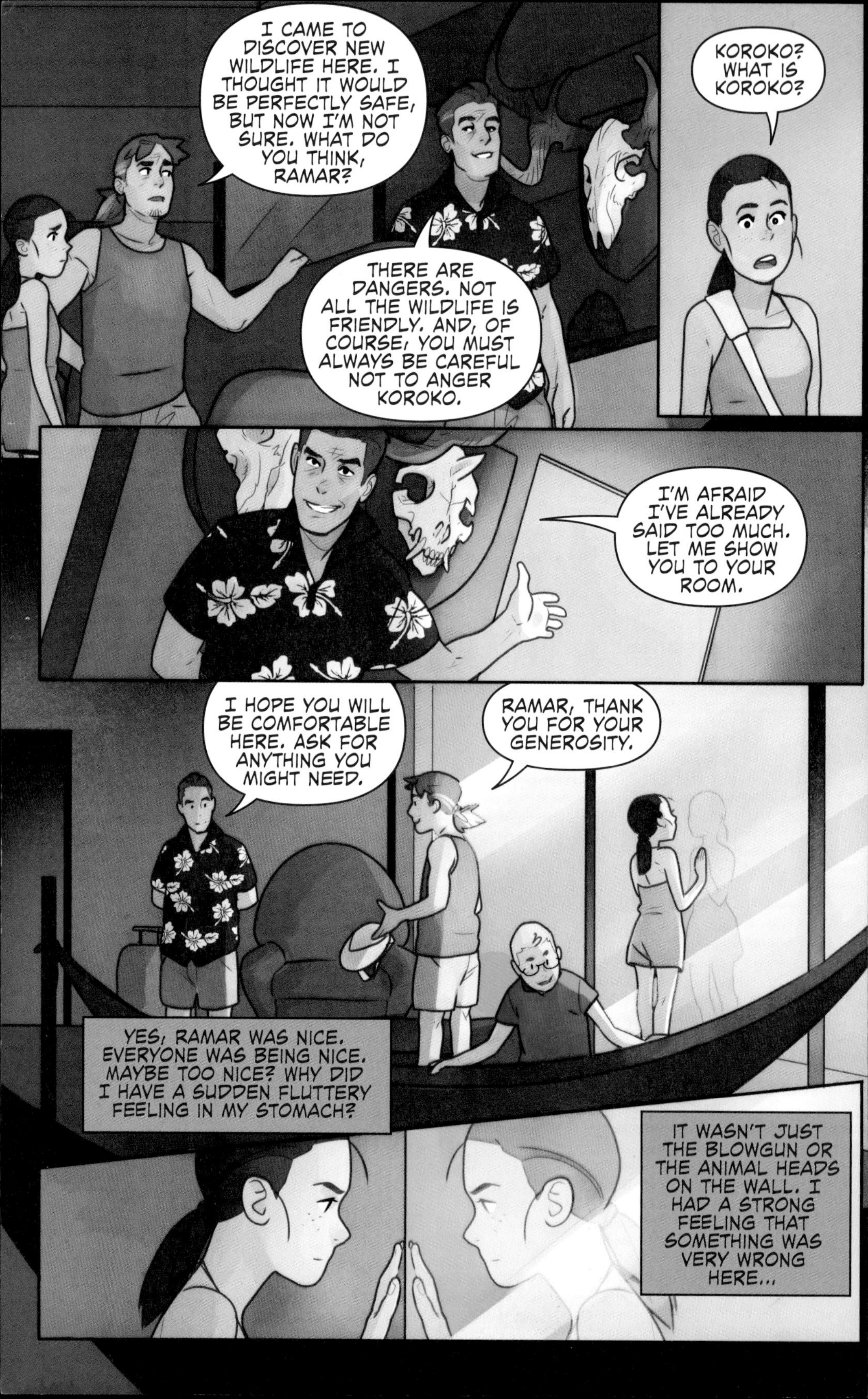
I CAME TO DISCOVER NEW WILDLIFE HERE. I THOUGHT IT WOULD BE PERFECTLY SAFE, BUT NOW I'M NOT SURE. WHAT DO YOU THINK, RAMAR?
THERE ARE DANGERS. NOT ALL THE WILDLIFE IS FRIENDLY. AND, OF COURSE, YOU MUST ALWAYS BE CAREFUL NOT TO ANGER KOROKO.
KOROKO? WHAT IS KOROKO?
I'M AFRAID I'VE ALREADY SAID TOO MUCH. LET ME SHOW YOU TO YOUR ROOM.
I HOPE YOU WILL BE COMFORTABLE HERE. ASK FOR ANYTHING YOU MIGHT NEED.
RAMAR, THANK YOU FOR YOUR GENEROSITY.
YES, RAMAR WAS NICE. EVERYONE WAS BEING NICE. MAYBE TOO NICE? WHY DID I HAVE A SUDDEN FLUTTERY FEELING IN MY STOMACH?
IT WASN'T JUST THE BLOWGUN OR THE ANIMAL HEADS ON THE WALL. I HAD A STRONG FEELING THAT SOMETHING WAS VERY WRONG HERE...

CHAPTER FOUR
YOU'D BETTER SUCK THE POISON OUT!
WE UNPACKED. THEN IT WAS TIME TO DO A LITTLE EXPLORING.
LET'S GO OUTSIDE. I SEE ANIMALS OUT THERE IN THE TALL GRASS.
TRY NOT TO FALL IN A HOLE, OKAY?
THE BACK YARD WAS SURROUNDED BY A TALL FENCE. IN THE TALL GRASS, CUTE LITTLE CREATURES POPPED THEIR HEADS UP.
THEY'RE ADORABLE! ARE THEY SOME KIND OF MICE?
WITH LONG EARS? HAHA. MAYBE THEY'RE MOUSE-RABBITS.

LOOK HOW TAME THEY ARE!
HAHA. THIS ONE IS LICKING MY HAND!
I'VE NEVER SEEN THIS SPECIES. I'LL GO GET MY CAMERA.
THIS ONE WANTS TO RACE. QUICK, GET IT ON VIDEO. THIS COULD GO VIRAL!
BENNY--BEING BENNY--SLIPPED AND FELL.
OOOOOF!

I FROZE AS AN UGLY-LOOKING SNAKE ROSE UP FROM THE TALL GRASS.
BENNY HOWLED AS THE SNAKE SANK ITS FANGS INTO HIS ARM.
CHOMP!
YEOWWWWWWW! IT *BIT* ME!!

UNCLE BILL CAME RUNNING. HE EXAMINED BENNY'S ARM.
OWWW. IT REALLY HURTS.
THAT'S A DEEP BITE. WE NEED TO TREAT IT.
RAMAR-- HE HAS A DEEP SNAKEBITE. IS THERE A DOCTOR?
A DOCTOR ON *MALA SUERTE?* YOU'VE GOT TO BE KIDDING.
LET ME SEE THAT BITE. OH... TOO BAD.

YOU'D BETTER SUCK OUT THE POISON...IF IT ISN'T TOO LATE.
TOO LATE?

THE BITE OF A SWAMP COBRA CARRIES A POWERFUL VENOM.
UNCLE BILL DIDN'T HESITATE. HE FRANTICALLY SUCKED THE VENOM FROM BENNY'S ARM AND SPIT IT ON THE FLOOR. BENNY TWISTED AND SQUIRMED IN PAIN.
SIT STILL, BENNY. I'VE ALMOST GOT IT.
HERE ARE SOME BANDAGES.
OHHH, I FEEL WEIRD.
YOU'D BETTER REST FOR A WHILE.
UNCLE BILL AND I WATCHED BENNY AS HE MOANED AND GROANED AND FINALLY FELL ASLEEP.
THIS WOULDN'T HAVE HAPPENED AT DISNEY WORLD.
STOP! DON'T REMIND ME OF THAT HORRIBLE LIE I TOLD YOUR PARENTS. WHAT WAS I THINKING?

BENNY IS SLEEPING NICELY, AT LEAST.
HE'LL BE OKAY. IT'S MARISSA NEWTON I'M WORRIED ABOUT.
WHERE IS SHE? WHY DIDN'T SHE ARRIVE? IF ONLY I COULD CALL HER. BUT THE PHONES ARE USELESS HERE.
WHILE WE WAITED FOR BENNY TO WAKE UP, UNCLE BILL TOOK OUT SOME MAPS TO SHOW ME.
THIS IS WHERE WE'LL START TOMORROW. IT'S CALLED THE *MIASMA*. IT MEANS ***SWAMP.***
WE CAN EXPLORE ALONG THE RIVER BANK. MAYBE WE'LL SEE MORE OF THOSE LITTLE MOUSE CREATURES. I DIDN'T GET ANY GOOD PHOTOS OF THEM.
SUDDENLY, BENNY BEGAN MAKING TERRIBLE NOISES IN HIS SLEEP.
WHY IS HE DOING THAT?! HE SOUNDS LIKE A WILD ANIMAL!
GRRRR RRRRR RRROWRRRR
CALM DOWN, KARLA. HE'S JUST SNORING.

BENNY DIDN'T WAKE UP 'TIL EVENING. BY THEN, WE WERE ALL STARVING.
HOW DO YOU FEEL, BENNY?
HUNGRY.
LET'S GO OUT AND SEE IF THE CAFÉ IS STILL OPEN.
BUT WHEN WE TRIED THE FRONT DOOR, WE HAD A SURPRISE.
IT'S LOCKED! THE FRONT DOOR IS LOCKED!
WE TRIED THE BACK DOORS, BUT THEY WERE LOCKED, TOO.
RAMAR? RAMAR? ARE YOU HERE?
HE'S GONE!
HE LOCKED US IN. WE'RE PRISONERS!

CHAPTER FIVE
DINNER FOR KOROKO
...TRAPPED IN THE HOUSE, THE HARLANS' SHOUTS FOR RAMAR WILL NOT BE HEARD. RAMAR IS FAR FROM THE VILLAGE, GUIDING A SMALL CANOE ALONG THE SANGRE RIVER THAT TWISTS THROUGH THE ISLAND SWAMPLAND...
BLASTED MOSQUITOS. AS BIG AS CANARIES. I'VE SWEATED THROUGH MY SHIRT IN THIS HEAT. THE SWAMP SMELLS SOUR AS DEATH. BUT I HAVE NO CHOICE...
IT'S SOMETHING I MUST DO, AS A FAITHFUL SERVANT.
FEEDING TIME AT THE ZOO.

SPLAAAAAASH
COME GET YOUR DINNER, KOROKO! I BROUGHT YOU A TASTY DINNER!

RRRROWWWWWWRRR
KOROKO!

RRRRROWWWWWRRRRR
RRRRRRIIIIIIIIIIPPPP
AS RAMAR LOOKS ON, THE MONSTER DEVOURS THE MEAL. DROOL RUNS DOWN KOROKO'S CHIN. CHICKEN GUTS DRIBBLE FROM HIS MONSTROUS JAWS.
CHOMP
CHOMP
DROOL CHOMP
CHOMP
DROOL URRRRP
URRRRP
CHOMP

THAT'S JUST AN APPETIZER, KOROKO. I HAVE DELICIOUS FRESH MEAT FOR YOU.
YOUR MEAL IS LOCKED UP IN MY HOUSE. I'M KEEPING IT FRESH FOR YOU.
RRRRRRRRRRRRR
I AM YOUR FRIEND, KOROKO. I ALWAYS BRING YOU YOUR FAVORITE FOOD.
SO YOU WILL BE MY FRIEND, TOO--YES?
RRRRRRRRRRRRRR
FOLLOW ME HOME, KOROKO. YOU WILL LIKE THE DINNER. THERE ARE THREE HUMANS FOR YOU. THE TWO SMALLER ONES ARE YOUNG AND TENDER! HAHA.

ALWAYS EAGER FOR FRESH HUMAN MEAT, THE MONSTER FOLLOWS RAMAR DOWN THE RIVER TOWARD THE VILLAGE.
CLOMP
CLOMMMP
CLOMMPP
KOROKO GRABS A SNACK OFF A LOW TREE LIMB.
CHIRRRP--??
THE MONSTER SWALLOWS THE BIRD WHOLE. RAMAR TREMBLES. HE'LL DO ANYTHING TO PLEASE THE HUNGRY BEAST. EVEN SACRIFICE KARLA, BENNY, AND UNCLE BILL.
A FISHERMAN AND HIS FAMILY SCREAM AT THE SIGHT OF THE APPROACHING MONSTER. THEY FLEE FOR THEIR LIVES.
AIIIIEEEEEEE!

THEY APPROACH THE VILLAGE. ALL WHO LIVE ON THE ISLAND KNOW KOROKO. AND ALL FEAR THE BEAST AND HIS HUNGER.
IT'S KOROKO! RUN!
RUN!
THE MONSTER IS HERE!
YAAAAAAIIIII!

RAMAR LEADS THE WAY TO HIS HOUSE. KOROKO BEGINS TO DROOL IN ANTICIPATION OF A BIG THREE-COURSE MEAL.
PREPARE YOURSELF FOR A FEAST, KOROKO. REMEMBER, I AM YOUR FRIEND. I WANT YOU TO ENJOY YOURSELF.
YOUR DINNER AWAITS BEHIND THIS DOOR.
I KNOW THEIR SCREAMS WILL MAKE THEM EVEN MORE DELICIOUS FOR YOU!
RAMAR PULLS OPEN THE DOOR...
...AND SCREAMS.
OH NOOOO! THE ROOM IS EMPTY! WHERE DID THEY GO?

THEY *ESCAPED!* THEY SMASHED THE GLASS DOORS AND ESCAPED!
DISAPPOINTED, KOROKO GOES INTO A ROARING RAGE.
RRRRRRRRRRRRRRR
NO! PLEASE! PUT ME DOWN! PUT ME *DOWN!*
HEEEEAVE!

NOOOOOOOOOOOOO!
THE MONSTER TAKES OUT HIS ANGER BY SMASHING WHATEVER HE CAN GRAB. THE VILLAGERS FLEE IN TERROR.
SOMEONE MADE KOROKO ANGRY. I FEEL SORRY FOR WHOEVER IT WAS.

CHAPTER SIX
NO SUCH THING AS MONSTERS
THE WET SAND--IT'S UP TO MY KNEES. HOW FAR ARE WE GOING TO RUN?
WE HAVE TO GET AWAY FROM THE VILLAGE.
IS THAT A CAVE? CAN WE CHECK IT OUT?
AT LEAST IT'S COOL IN HERE. I'M SWEATING LIKE A PIG.
THEY HAVE THIS NEW THING CALLED DEODORANT.
HAVE YOU HEARD OF IT?
DON'T START UP, YOU TWO. WE ARE IN MAJOR TROUBLE. WE HAVE TO THINK!
ARE WE GOING TO HIDE IN HERE?
WE'RE NOT GOING TO HIDE.
HUH?

WE'RE GOING TO DO OUR WORK. I CAME HERE TO DISCOVER NEW ANIMALS AND BECOME FAMOUS.
BUT THAT MAN LOCKED US UP AND--
I DON'T KNOW WHAT HIS PROBLEM WAS, BUT WE'RE DONE WITH HIM. WE CAN WORK OUT OF THIS CAVE UNTIL--
KOFF KOFF
HEY-- I HEARD SOMETHING.
I HEARD IT, TOO. WAS IT SOME KIND OF ANIMAL?
SOMETHING IS MOVING AROUND BACK THERE. WE'RE NOT ALONE!
HELLO? HELLO?
IS SOMEONE THERE? WHO'S THERE?

MARISSA? YOU'RE *HERE?!*
BILL!
I'M SO GLAD TO SEE YOU. I'VE BEEN HIDING HERE SINCE I ARRIVED.
BUT--BUT--WHY?
THE ISLANDERS--THEY SMILE AND PRETEND TO BE WELCOMING. BUT THEY'RE *NOT.*
THEY DON'T WANT US HERE. WE HAVE TO LEAVE, BILL. WE'RE NOT SAFE. WE--
TAKE A BREATH. CALM DOWN, MARISSA.
I CAN'T. DO YOU KNOW WHAT THE VILLAGERS CALL THIS PLACE? *THE ISLAND OF UNENDING SCREAMS.*

HUH? EXCEPT FOR A GUY NAMED RAMAR, THE PEOPLE HERE ALL SEEM NICE.
THEY'RE NOT NICE. THEY ALL LIVE IN TERROR. IT'S LIKE A LIVING HORROR MOVIE.
OH *NO!* DID YOU HEAR THAT? SOMEONE HAS FOUND US!
I DIDN'T HEAR ANYTHING. YOU CAN'T LET THESE RUMORS SCARE YOU, MARISSA.
YES, I CAN. I HEARD TALK OF A MONSTER-- HALF-HUMAN, HALF-BEAST. THEY SAID HE RULES THE WHOLE ISLAND.
A MONSTER? SERIOUSLY?!
MARISSA, WE ARE SCIENTISTS. YOU KNOW THERE'S NO SUCH THING AS MONSTERS.
I KNOW WHAT I KNOW. I KNOW WHAT WAS WAITING FOR ME HERE WHEN I ARRIVED...

"WHEN I STEPPED OFF THE BOAT, VILLAGERS WERE THERE TO MEET ME. EVERYTHING SEEMED FINE AT FIRST. ALL SMILES AND WELCOMES. MEN HELPED ME BRING MY BAGS ON DECK, AND MY SCIENTIFIC GEAR. A WOMAN GAVE ME FLOWERS!
"BUT WHEN I STARTED TO THE INN, I LOOKED BACK. I DIDN'T SEE MY BAGS OR MY EQUIPMENT.
"I WENT RUNNING BACK. I SHOUTED, 'WHERE ARE ALL MY BELONGINGS?' EVERYONE JUST SHRUGGED. THEIR SMILES HAD TURNED EVIL."

"SUDDENLY, SOMEONE SCREAMED. THE VILLAGERS BACKED AWAY. I FROZE AS A MONSTROUS ALLIGATOR BURST FROM THE WATER, SNAPPING ITS ENORMOUS JAWS."
OHHHH... HELP!
"THE GATOR LOWERED ITS HEAD AND, SHAKING OFF WATER, RACED TOWARD ME. I SPUN AWAY--AND RAN!
"NO ONE MADE A MOVE TO STOP IT. WHY DID IT SUDDENLY COME LEAPING UP? WHY DID IT CHOOSE ME TO ATTACK? QUESTIONS I TRIED TO ANSWER AS I RAN FOR MY LIFE."

"I FLED THROUGH THE VILLAGE AND INTO THE SWAMP. GRUNTING AND SNAPPING ITS JAWS, THE GATOR STAYED WITH ME STEP FOR STEP. I GASPED FOR BREATH. I DIDN'T KNOW HOW MUCH FURTHER I COULD RUN.

"MY LEGS WERE GIVING OUT. MY WHOLE BODY THROBBED WITH PAIN. I SHRIEKED WHEN I FELT JAGGED TEETH TIGHTEN OVER MY ANKLE.
"WITH A DESPERATE BURST OF STRENGTH, I PULLED FREE. I DOVE INTO A LOW CAVE CUT INTO THE ANCIENT SWAMP TREES.
"THE BEAST CONTINUED TO SNAP AT ME. BUT I WAS SAFE. THE CAVE MOUTH WAS TOO LOW FOR HIM TO REACH ME."

I DIDN'T KNOW WHAT TO THINK. DID THE VILLAGERS SEND THAT BEAST AFTER ME? WHAT HAPPENED TO MY BELONGINGS?
I'VE BEEN HIDING IN CAVES EVER SINCE, HOPING I'D FIND YOU.
RRRRRRRRRROOOOOOORRRRRR
WHAT'S *THAT?*
WAS THAT...THE *MONSTER?*
JUST TROPICAL THUNDER, BENNY.
ARE YOU SURE?
HEY, UNCLE BILL. SOMETHING WEIRD...SOME-THING WEIRD IS HAPPENING TO ME!

CHAPTER SEVEN
SOMETHING WEIRD IS HAPPENING TO BENNY
MY BROTHER HELD HIS ARM UP AND I GASPED. IT WAS HUGE. IT HAD SWOLLEN UP LIKE A BIG HAM!
LOOK. LOOK AT MY ARM!
OH NOOO.
WEIRD...
THIS IS NOT GOOD. I THOUGHT I SUCKED ALL THE SNAKE VENOM OUT.
AND LOOK. BENNY'S ARM IS SPROUTING HAIR. HOW STRANGE...
NOOOO. WHAT IS HAPPENING TO ME?!
WE DON'T HAVE ANY MEDICINE. WE'LL HAVE TO JUST WAIT AND WATCH IT CAREFULLY.
I...I FEEL STRANGE. LIKE MY INSIDES ARE ALL JITTERY.

WE HAVE TO GET HIM TO A DOCTOR. IMMEDIATELY.
WE CAN'T. THERE ARE NO DOCTORS ON THE ISLAND.
WE CAN'T STAY HERE, DR. HARLAN. BENNY NEEDS TREATMENT.
THE VENOM MAY WORK ITS WAY THROUGH HIM. THE SWELLING WILL PROBABLY GO DOWN.
LOOK AT BENNY'S SHOULDER. HIS SHOULDER IS SPROUTING HAIR, TOO!
WE JUST ARRIVED. WE'VE COME TOO FAR TO SACRIFICE OUR WORK. THIS TRIP WILL MAKE US FAMOUS!
YOU DON'T WANT TO SACRIFICE YOUR NEPHEW JUST TO BECOME FAMOUS, DO YOU? WE HAVE TO GET BACK TO THE BOAT.
PLEASE-- UNCLE BILL! LOOK AT BENNY'S ARM. IT'S TOTALLY GROSS!
OKAY. OKAY. WE'LL WAIT 'TIL NIGHT. THEN WE CAN SNEAK BACK TO THE BOAT AND GET OUT OF HERE.

THE AFTERNOON SEEMED TO STRETCH ON AND ON. MY POOR BROTHER SAT AT THE BACK OF THE CAVE, FEELING SICK. I WATCHED HIM CAREFULLY. HIS OTHER ARM WAS SWELLING UP, TOO.
AS SOON AS IT WAS DARK, WE CREPT OUT OF THE CAVE AND BEGAN TO MAKE OUR WAY THROUGH THE SWAMP TOWARD THE VILLAGE.
WHOOO WHOOO
UNCLE BILL STOPPED US WHEN HE HEARD A BIRD CRY.
HE INSISTED ON TAKING PHOTOS OF IT.
I DON'T BELIEVE IT. IS THAT A TWO-HEADED OWL?
AMAZING. WHAT A SHAME TO MISS ALL THESE INCREDIBLE ANIMALS.

LOOK AT MY ARMS. THEY'RE COVERED IN FUR NOW! I FEEL SO... WEIRD.
THE CREW WILL BE WAITING ON THE BOAT. WE'LL GET YOU TO A DOCTOR, BENNY.
MAYBE I SHOULD CUT BENNY'S ARM AND SUCK OUT MORE VENOM FROM THE BITE.
LET'S JUST GET HIM ON THE BOAT AND HURRY AWAY FROM THIS ISLAND.
I'M SO SORRY. THE OTHER SCIENTISTS WARNED ME NOT TO COME HERE. BUT I WAS STUBBORN.
THERE'S THE DOCK UP AHEAD. ALMOST TO THE BOAT, BENNY.

BUT WHEN WE GOT TO THE DOCK...
OH *NOOOOOO!* OUR BOAT--!

CHAPTER EIGHT
CURSED!
SOMEONE DID THIS. SOMEONE SET OUR BOAT ON FIRE AND SENT IT OFF INTO THE WATER.
BUT...WHY? WHO WOULD DO THAT TO US?
WE'RE NOT SAFE. SOMEONE WANTS TO KEEP US HERE.
WE HAVE TO CALL FOR ANOTHER BOAT.
WE CAN'T. REMEMBER? THERE'S NO PHONE SERVICE ON THE ISLAND.
BUT...BUT...WE CAN'T LIVE HERE FOREVER!
DON'T WORRY. WHEN OUR LAB PARTNERS DISCOVER WE ARE MISSING, THEY WILL SEND ANOTHER BOAT.
LOOK AT ME. MY BODY IS STILL CHANGING. HOW CAN I BE A MOVIE STAR LOOKING LIKE BIGFOOT?

OH YUCK. THE FUR--IT'S SPROUTING ON HIS NECK!
WE HAVE TO TAKE OUR CHANCES IN THE VILLAGE. MAYBE SOMEONE WILL KNOW WHAT TO DO.
WE WANDERED DOWN THE NARROW DIRT STREET PAST HOUSES AND SHOPS. IT WAS LATE. EVERYONE WAS INDOORS.
A MAN WALKED BY CARRYING A FISHERMAN'S NET. UNCLE BILL STOPPED HIM.
EXCUSE ME. CAN YOU HELP US? LOOK AT MY NEPHEW. HE--
SWAMP COBRA? A SWAMP COBRA BITE? *STAY AWAY!* IT'S *CONTAGIOUS!*
WE WATCHED IN SHOCK AS THE MAN TOOK OFF RUNNING.

YOU MEAN I'M GOING TO SWELL UP AND GROW FUR, TOO?
NO. DON'T LISTEN TO THAT GUY.
HE WAS JUST SUPERSTITIOUS. SNAKE VENOM CAN'T MOVE FROM PERSON TO PERSON.
A MAN CAME WALKING OUT OF A SMALL TAVERN. HE STOPPED WHEN HE SAW US. AND HE SQUINTED HARD AT MY BROTHER.
SNAKE BITE?
YES. BENNY WAS BITTEN BY A SWAMP COBRA. DO YOU KNOW ANYTHING ABOUT IT?
MY NAME IS DR. MABUSE. I KNOW A LITTLE ABOUT MEDICINE.
YOU'RE A DOCTOR?
NO. A VETERINARIAN.

WE HAD NO CHOICE. WE NEEDED HELP. WE FOLLOWED DR. MABUSE TO HIS SMALL SHACK.
THE WALLS WERE COVERED WITH MOUNTED ANIMAL FEET. I GASPED SEEING THEM ALL.
I HUNT WILD PIGS. I MOUNT THEIR FEET ON MY WALL AS TROPHIES OF MY HUNT.
WHAT KIND OF VET LIKES TO KILL ANIMALS? I FELT SICK. I WANTED TO LEAVE. BUT POOR BENNY WAS SUFFERING.
HAVE YOU EVER TREATED THIS?
YES. I TREATED A HORSE WITH THIS KIND OF SNAKEBITE.
UNFORTUNATELY, IT SWELLED UP AND DIED.
NOW I REALLY WANTED TO GET OUT OF THERE. BUT DR. MABUSE ALREADY HAD A GRIP ON BENNY'S ARM.
LET ME EXAMINE THE BITE CLOSELY IN THE LIGHT. I HAVE TO BRUSH THE FUR AWAY TO SEE...
AFTER A FEW SECONDS, THE DOCTOR'S EYES BULGED AND HE LET OUT A SCREAM.
OH, MY HEAVENS!

MABUSE JUMPED BACK AND RAISED BOTH HANDS IN THE AIR IN HORROR.
THE SNAKEBITE-- IT'S NOT YOUR PROBLEM. YOU ARE CURSED! *CURSED!* GET OUT OF HERE! GET *OUT* OF MY HOUSE!
YOU ARE *CURSED!* YOU ARE *DOOMED!* GET AWAY! GET AWAY FROM ME!
WE RAN THROUGH THE VILLAGE, INTO THE SWAMP. WE DIDN'T STOP 'TIL WE WERE BACK NEAR THE CAVE. I FELT FRIGHTENED AND CONFUSED.
HE'S SUPERSTITIOUS, TOO. RIGHT, UNCLE BILL?
EVERYONE HERE SEEMS TO BE SUPERSTITIOUS. THERE'S NO SUCH THING AS A CURSE.
ARE YOU SURE?
I'M A SCIENTIST. I BELIEVE IN WHAT'S REAL. WE'RE GOING TO GET YOU CURED, BENNY.

CHAPTER NINE
BENNY AND THE CRAB MONSTER
WE SLEPT RESTLESSLY. BENNY KEPT MAKING GROWLING NOISES IN HIS SLEEP. I WAS TERRIFIED. WAS HE REALLY TURNING INTO SOME KIND OF ANIMAL?
I OPENED MY EYES IN THE MORNING AND HOPED BENNY WOULD BE BACK TO NORMAL. BUT NO. HIS CHEST WAS SWELLING UP. HIS ARMS AND SHOULDERS WERE COVERED IN FUR.
I HAVE AN IDEA. IT CAME TO ME DURING THE NIGHT.
PLEASE--TELL US.
I'VE BEEN STUDYING YOUR MAPS, DOCTOR HARLAN. I DON'T KNOW HOW WE MISSED IT BEFORE. THERE'S ANOTHER VILLAGE...
REALLY? MAYBE THE PEOPLE THERE ARE FRIENDLIER.
MAYBE SOMEONE WILL HELP US ONTO A BOAT SO WE CAN ESCAPE THIS ISLAND.
SEE? WE'LL HAVE TO FOLLOW THE RIVER THROUGH THE SWAMP TO THE OTHER SIDE OF THE ISLAND.
WILL IT BE SAFE?
SAFER THAN STAYING HERE IN THE VILLAGE.

A HOT, STEAMY DAY IN THE SWAMP. WE STARTED WALKING ALONG THE RIVER BANK...
HOW DO YOU FEEL, BENNY?
RRRRR. HOW DO YOU *THINK* I FEEL?
TRY TO KEEP YOUR SPIRITS UP. WE'RE GOING TO GET YOU HELP.
JUST THINK. WHEN YOU'RE A BIG MOVIE STAR AND YOU WRITE YOUR BIOGRAPHY, YOU'LL HAVE AN ***AWESOME*** STORY TO TELL!
OH, SURE. I'LL BE A STAR. A STAR IN A *KING KONG* MOVIE! ***GRROWWLLL.*** I'M SUDDENLY ***SO*** HUNGRY...
WITHOUT WARNING, BENNY GRABBED A LIZARD UP FROM THE GRASS...
AND SHOVED IT INTO HIS MOUTH!
CHOMMMP!
CHOMMP!
CHOMP!
CHOMP!
CHOMP!

OH NOOOO! WHAT DID YOU JUST DO?!
I COULDN'T HELP MYSELF. I WAS HUNGRY.
I FELT A SHIVER OF FEAR. WAS BENNY GETTING DANGEROUS?
UURRRRRRP!
IT'S OKAY, KARLA. BENNY'S GONNA TRY TO KEEP IT TOGETHER 'TIL WE FIND AN ANTIDOTE. RIGHT, BENNY?
KEEP IT TOGETHER? ARE YOU KIDDING ME? LOOK AT ME!
UNCLE BILL STARTED TO REPLY. BUT HE STOPPED WHEN WE HEARD SHRILL SCREAMS.
YAAAAAAIIIIIIIII!
THE SCREAMS SOUNDED DESPERATE. WE WENT RUNNING TOWARD THEM.
SOUNDS LIKE KIDS!

HELLLLP! HELP US!
IT'S CRUSHING ME!!
WHAT IS THAT THING?!
I DON'T BELIEVE IT!

WAS IT A GIANT CRAB MONSTER? SOME KIND OF MUTANT SNAPPING TURTLE?
UNCLE BILL AND DR. NEWTON WENT RUNNING TO HELP THE KIDS.
BE CAREFUL! WATCH OUT!
UNCLE BILL AND DR. NEWTON BATTLED TO FREE THE TWO KIDS. THE FIERCE CREATURE SNAPPED AND CLAWED AND REFUSED TO GIVE UP...

NOOOOOO! LET GO OF THEM! LET GO!
I GASPED AS BENNY SUDDENLY TOOK OFF, RUNNING TOWARD THE CRAB MONSTER.
RRRRRRRRRROWWWRRR!
BENNY-- COME BACK! WHAT ARE YOU DOING?!
ROARING LIKE A FURIOUS BEAST, MY BROTHER LEAPT ONTO THE CRAB MONSTER. BENNY BEGAN TEARING AND PUNCHING THE CREATURE WITH HIS HUGE FUR-COVERED FISTS.
RRRRROWWWWWR!

STARTLED BY BENNY'S ATTACK, THE GIANT CREATURE LOST ITS GRIP. THE HUGE CLAWS DROPPED OPEN, FREEING THE TWO KIDS, UNCLE BILL, AND DR. NEWTON.
WE ALL WATCHED IN SHOCK AS THE CRAB CREATURE SCRABBLED AWAY, INTO THE TREES...
WHOOOAH. BENNY--YOU BEAT HIM!
WHEW. THAT WAS A CLOSE ONE.
THAT CREATURE WAS STRONG.
BUT NOT AS STRONG AS BENNY!
YOU...YOU SAVED OUR LIVES!
WE THOUGHT... WE THOUGHT WE WERE DEAD MEAT.

WHO ARE YOU? WHAT ARE YOU DOING HERE? WHY DID THAT THING ATTACK YOU?
MY NAME IS HANNAH WOODSON. HE'S MY BROTHER, MARCUS.
WE WERE TRYING TO GET TO KOROKO VILLAGE. BUT THAT THING--
THAT THING SURPRISED US. IT CAME FROM OUT OF NOWHERE.
IF YOU HADN'T COME ALONG...
YOU WERE SO BRAVE. AND STRONG. YOUR ARMS...ARE YOU--?
I'M A FREAK.
YOU'RE NOT A FREAK, BENNY. DON'T SAY THAT.
BENNY WAS BITTEN BY A SNAKE. HE'S HAD A BAD REACTION.

DID YOU SAY YOU WERE HEADED TO KOROKO VILLAGE? THE VILLAGE ON THE OTHER SIDE OF THE ISLAND?
YES. MARCUS AND I HAVE TO GET THERE.
YOU'RE GOING ALONE? WHERE ARE YOUR PARENTS?
WELL...
THEY WERE CAPTURED.
CAPTURED? WHO CAPTURED THEM?
WE WAITED. BUT HANNAH AND MARCUS WOULDN'T ANSWER THE QUESTION. MARCUS CHANGED THE SUBJECT.
WHERE ARE YOU ALL GOING? WHY ARE YOU IN THE SWAMP?
WE'RE GOING TO KOROKO VILLAGE, TOO. WE HAVE TO FIND HELP FOR BENNY.
DID THAT FUR JUST GROW ON YOU?
YES. AND I'M GROWING AND GROWING. I CAN FEEL MY SKIN STRETCHING. IT'S LIKE... MY BODY IS OUT OF CONTROL.
LET'S GO TOGETHER.

A BOAT. IS IT YOURS?
WE FOUND IT HIDDEN IN THE TALL GRASS. IT'S BIG ENOUGH FOR ALL SIX OF US.
UNCLE BILL, WHY DO YOU LOOK SO UNHAPPY?
I CAN'T BELIEVE WE DIDN'T SNAP ANY PHOTOS OF THAT GIANT CRAB. IT WOULD HAVE BEEN A SENSATION BACK HOME.
IT'S HARD TO TAKE PHOTOS WHEN YOU'RE BEING SQUEEZED TO DEATH.
*ROWWWR.* CAN WE STOP TALKING AND GO? THIS FUR IS ITCHING LIKE CRAZY!
SO, WE SET OFF ON THE RIVER WITH THESE TWO KIDS. THE SUN WAS STILL HIGH IN THE SKY. THE WATER WAS SHALLOW AND CALM. BUT I COULDN'T RELAX FOR A MOMENT. SOMETHING TROUBLED ME. WHO HAD CAPTURED THEIR PARENTS? AND WHY WERE THEY KEEPING IT SECRET?

CHAPTER TEN
SWEPT AWAY
THE RIVER TWISTED THROUGH THE SWAMP. OUR BOAT BOBBED ON THE BROWN WATER AS THE CURRENT CARRIED US FASTER.
STRANGE BIRDS SOARED ABOVE US. UNCLE BILL TRIED TO SNAP PHOTOS OF THEM.
THEY LOOK SO PRIMITIVE. LIKE THE RAPTORS FROM DINOSAUR DAYS.
I TRIED TO BE FRIENDLY WITH MARCUS AND HANNAH. BUT THEY WOULDN'T TALK MUCH...
DID YOUR PARENTS COME HERE FOR WORK?
NOT REALLY.
HOW LONG HAVE YOU BEEN ON *MALA SUERTE*? WHEN WERE YOUR PARENTS CAPTURED?
HARD TO SAY.

THE RIVER GREW WIDER AND THE CURRENT CARRIED US UPHILL. I STARED AT BENNY. I COULD BARELY RECOGNIZE MY POOR BROTHER.
BENNY, HOW DO YOU FEEL?
HUNNNNGRY.
BENNY KEPT LEANING OVER THE SIDE AND TRAILING HIS HAND IN THE RIVER WATER.
WHY ARE YOU DOING THAT? YOU'RE TIPPING THE BOAT.
HUNNNGRY.
BENNY, YOU'RE GOING TO TIP US OVER. WHAT ARE YOU DOING?
I CRIED OUT AS MY BROTHER GRABBED A FISH FROM THE RIVER.
GOT IT!

WE ALL GROANED AS BENNY DEVOURED IT LIKE AN ANIMAL.
YUCK.
OHH. SICK.
CHOMP CHOMP URRP SLURRP!
BENNY HAD A PLEASED SMILE ON HIS FACE AS HE TOSSED THE FISH BONES INTO THE WATER.
URRRRRP!
KARLA, YOUR BROTHER IS TOTALLY GROSS.
BENNY CAN'T HELP IT. HE NEEDS A DOCTOR.
HA. HE NEEDS A ZOOKEEPER! YOU NEED TO PUT HIM ON A LEASH!
THAT'S NOT FUNNY. WE TOLD YOU. HE HAD AN ALLERGIC REACTION TO A SNAKEBITE.
BE CAREFUL. I'D BE AFRAID OF A BENNY BITE! HAHA.
WHY ARE YOU BEING SO CRUEL TO HIM? DO YOU HAVE ANY IDEA HOW SCARED HE IS?

AS WE ARGUED, WE DIDN'T NOTICE THE RIVER HAD CHANGED. THE CURRENT PULLED US HARD FROM SIDE TO SIDE. THE BROWN WATER GAVE WAY TO DARK BLUE, WITH WHITE FOAM BEATING AGAINST OUR SMALL BOAT.
HEY--WHERE DID THESE RAPIDS COME FROM?
THE RUSHING WATER RAISED OUR LITTLE BOAT HIGH, THEN SENT US CRASHING DOWN.
WHOOOOOOAAAH!
HOLD ON TIGHT TO THE SIDES, EVERYONE!
BUT BENNY DIDN'T LISTEN. HE LEANED OVER AND REACHED INTO THE WATER TO GRAB ANOTHER FISH.
HUNNNNGRY.

WE ALL SHRIEKED IN HORROR AS BENNY PLUNGED OVER THE SIDE.
MY HEART STOPPED. I FROZE IN HORROR. THE RAPIDS WERE CARRYING BENNY AWAY. I GASPED AS DR. NEWTON AND UNCLE BILL LEAPED IN TO SAVE HIM.
OHH NOOOOOO!
NOOOOOOOOOOO!
AIIIIEEEEEEE!

HELLLLP. THE CURRENT... I CAN'T...
I COULDN'T BREATHE. I SAW THAT THE ROARING WATER WAS ABOUT TO DRAG BENNY OVER THE STEEP FALLS.
NOOOOOO! PLEASE!
WE GOT YOU!
STRUGGLING AGAINST THE POUNDING CURRENT, THEY DRAGGED MY BROTHER BACK TO THE SIDE OF THE BOAT.

BENNY WAS GASPING FOR BREATH, WATER POURING DOWN HIS FACE. I GRABBED HIM BY THE SHOULDERS AND HELPED PULL HIM BACK INTO THE BOAT.
HE FLOPPED ONTO HIS BELLY AND DIDN'T MOVE. HANGING ONTO THE SIDE FOR DEAR LIFE, I RAISED MY EYES-- AND SAW UNCLE BILL AND DR. NEWTON IN TROUBLE.
THE CURRENT... IT'S TOO STRONG...
PULLING ME...I CAN'T FIGHT IT...
I SCREAMED AS I WATCHED THEM PULLED TO THE FALLS. CLOSER...CLOSER...
NOOOOOOOOOO!

YAAAAAAIIIIIIIII!!
OH NO, OH NO, THIS CAN'T BE HAPPENING.
THEY WERE GONE.

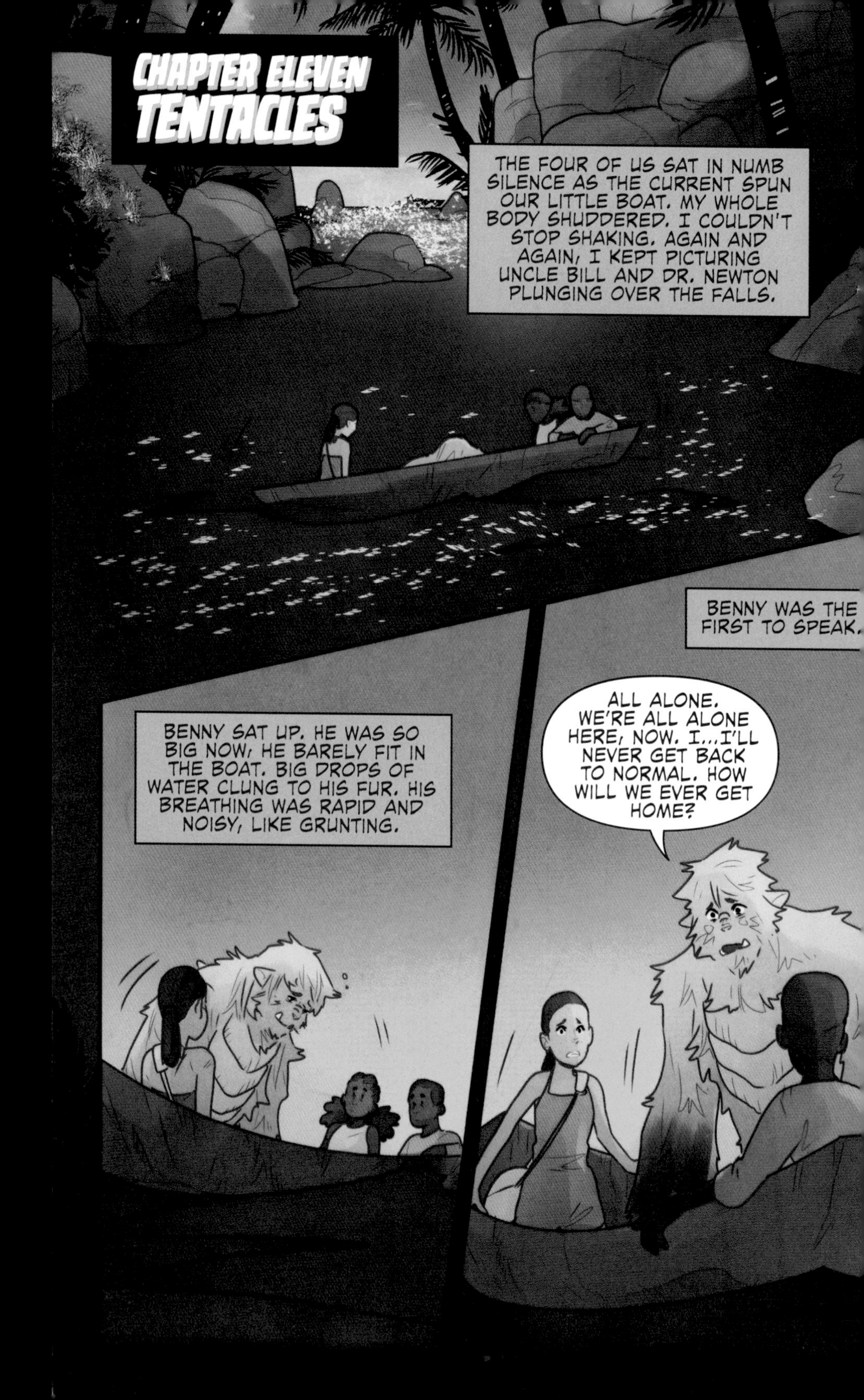
CHAPTER ELEVEN
TENTACLES
THE FOUR OF US SAT IN NUMB SILENCE AS THE CURRENT SPUN OUR LITTLE BOAT. MY WHOLE BODY SHUDDERED. I COULDN'T STOP SHAKING. AGAIN AND AGAIN, I KEPT PICTURING UNCLE BILL AND DR. NEWTON PLUNGING OVER THE FALLS.
BENNY SAT UP. HE WAS SO BIG NOW, HE BARELY FIT IN THE BOAT. BIG DROPS OF WATER CLUNG TO HIS FUR. HIS BREATHING WAS RAPID AND NOISY, LIKE GRUNTING.
BENNY WAS THE FIRST TO SPEAK.
ALL ALONE. WE'RE ALL ALONE HERE, NOW. I...I'LL NEVER GET BACK TO NORMAL. HOW WILL WE EVER GET HOME?

I HUGGED MYSELF TIGHTLY TO TRY TO STOP THE SHIVERS. I DIDN'T HAVE AN ANSWER FOR MY BROTHER. HOW WOULD WE EVER SURVIVE ON OUR OWN ON THIS UNFRIENDLY ISLAND?
WE HAVE ONLY ONE HOPE. OUR PARENTS. IF WE CAN RESCUE THEM...
BUT WE DON'T KNOW IF THEY ARE STILL ALIVE. KOROKO--
BEFORE MARCUS COULD FINISH HIS SENTENCE, A DEAFENING ROAR SHOOK THE BOAT...SHOOK THE TREES...SENT THE WATER CRASHING INTO OUR BOAT.
RRRRRRRROOOOOOORRRRR
OH, WOW. HE MUST BE NEARBY.
WHAT *WAS* THAT?
IT'S KOROKO.
WHO IS KOROKO? *TELL* US!

THE CURRENT WAS CARRYING US INTO DARKNESS. TREE LIMBS TWINED OVER US, NEARLY BLOCKING OUT THE SUNLIGHT. THE SWAMP AIR GREW STICKY AND DAMP. MY WHOLE BODY STARTED TO ITCH.
DON'T YOU KNOW? DON'T YOU KNOW ABOUT THE SWAMP MONSTER?
BEFORE I COULD SPEAK, SOMETHING BUMPED THE BOAT HARD. WE ALL SCREAMED AS ENORMOUS TENTACLES REACHED UP FROM BELOW THE WATER.
AAAAAAAA!
WAS IT A GIANT SQUID? AN OCTOPUS? THE MONSTROUS TENTACLES CURLED OVER US AND STARTED TO PULL US DOWN.
WE'RE ALL GOING TO *DROWN!*
NOOOOOOOO!

SPLLLLUUUUSSSSSSSSH
WE HIT HARD AND WENT DOWN FAST. THE MURKY RIVER WATER ROSE UP AROUND US.
THROUGH THE MURKY WATER, I SAW BENNY BATTLING THE GIANT SQUID CREATURE THAT HAD PULLED US DOWN.
I KICKED AWAY FROM THE BOAT AND PULLED MYSELF TO THE SURFACE.
KARLA? ARE YOU OKAY? MARCUS HASN'T COME UP YET!

MARCUS? THANK GOODNESS. YOU'RE OKAY!
=COUGH COUGH= YUCK. I SWALLOWED A GALLON OF RIVER WATER.
BUT... WHERE'S BENNY?
RRRRRR. I TAUGHT THAT GRABBY CREATURE A LESSON!
WE SWAM TO SHORE. A FEW MINUTES LATER, WE WERE WALKING OVER THE SOGGY SAND AND THROUGH TALL SWAMP GRASS, TOWARD KOROKO VILLAGE.
BENNY, I CAN'T BELIEVE YOU RIPPED THAT TENTACLE OFF THE CREATURE.
I HAVE TO BE HONEST. I'M SERIOUSLY SCARED OF BENNY. LOOK AT HIM.
I'M SCARED OF MYSELF! I'M NEVER GONNA BE NORMAL.
I'M NEVER GONNA BE A STAR. NEVER!
BUT YOU SAVED US, BENNY. YOU'RE A STAR TO US!

WE MUST BE GETTING CLOSE TO THE VILLAGE. I JUST KEEP PRAYING OUR PARENTS ARE OKAY.
YOU DIDN'T FINISH TELLING US ABOUT KOROKO, HANNAH.
HOW COULD YOU COME TO *MALA SUERTE* AND NOT KNOW ABOUT KOROKO? KOROKO IS A ***MONSTER.*** HE RULES THE ISLAND.
YOU MEAN LIKE A MONSTER IN A HORROR MOVIE?
ONLY ***WE'RE*** IN THE MOVIE AND HE'S ***REAL!***
MY FAMILY DIDN'T MEAN TO COME HERE. OUR BOAT LET US OFF ON THE WRONG ISLAND. THE WHOLE THING WAS A TERRIBLE MISTAKE.
WE WERE TRYING TO GET AWAY. BUT OUR BOAT LEFT WITHOUT US. AND KOROKO GRABBED OUR PARENTS AND TOOK THEM AWAY.
WHY??
DON'T YOU KNOW ***ANY-THING??*** KOROKO IS A CARNIVORE. HE ***EATS PEOPLE!***

CHAPTER TWELVE
WHO WILL HE EAT?
WE REACHED THE VILLAGE AND GASPED IN SHOCK. THE HOUSES WERE EMPTY. THE SHOPS WERE DARK AND DESERTED. NO ONE ON THE STREET.
I KEEP STEPPING INTO BIG HOLES IN THE SAND.
THOSE AREN'T HOLES. THOSE ARE KOROKO FOOTPRINTS.
THE VILLAGE HAD BEEN ABANDONED.
NO ONE HERE. DID THEY ALL RUN FROM KOROKO?
OR DID HE EAT THEM ALL?
THERE'S NO ONE TO HELP US. NO ONE.
JUST PRAY THAT MY PARENTS ARE STILL ALIVE. THEY ARE OUR ONLY HOPE.

HANNAH POINTED TO A ROW OF LOW BUILDINGS TUCKED BEHIND A THICKET OF TREES.
ARE THOSE SMALL HOUSES?
NO. LOOK. THEY'RE CAGES.
WE CROSSED THE ABANDONED MARKET SQUARE AND CREPT CLOSE TO THEM.
THEY'RE LIKE ZOO CAGES. BUT...THERE ARE PEOPLE INSIDE THEM.
OH, WOW. DON'T YOU SEE? IT'S NOT A ZOO. IT'S KOROKO'S *PANTRY.* THIS IS WHERE HE STORES HIS FOOD!
THE SAD FACES OF KOROKO'S PRISONERS STARED OUT AT US FROM THE CAGES AS WE WALKED PAST.
HOW COME THERE AREN'T ANY GUARDS?
I GUESS THERE'S NO NEED. EVERYONE IS GONE. WHO WOULD STEAL HIS FOOD?
WE HURRIED ALONG THE CAGES. HANNAH AND MARCUS SEARCHED DESPERATELY FOR THEIR PARENTS. BUT NO SIGN OF THEM.
I FEEL SICK. DID KOROKO EAT THEM ALREADY?
DON'T SAY THAT, MARCUS. PLEASE. I...I CAN'T EVEN IMAGINE...

ANOTHER DEAFENING ROAR SHOOK THE GROUND. MY HEART JUMPED INTO MY MOUTH. I STOPPED AND GRABBED BENNY'S ARM. I HEARD THE HEAVY *THUD* OF FOOTSTEPS.
THE MONSTER. HE SOUNDS CLOSE!
WE WERE NEARLY TO THE LAST CAGE WHEN VOICES RANG OUT.
HANNAH! MARCUS? YOU'RE HERE?
YOU'VE *FOUND* US!
MOM! DAD! OH, THANK GOODNESS! YOU'RE OKAY!
I FELT SO HAPPY FOR HANNAH AND MARCUS. WHAT A WONDERFUL REUNION! THEY ALL TRIED TO HUG, BUT IT WAS HARD THROUGH THE WOODEN CAGE BARS.

ANOTHER SURPRISE MADE ME CRY OUT IN SHOCK. TWO OTHER PRISONERS IN THE CAGE. UNCLE BILL AND MARISSA NEWTON!
I DON'T *BELIEVE IT!*
YOU--YOU'RE HERE? YOU'RE OKAY?
SOMEHOW, WE SURVIVED OUR PLUNGE DOWN THE WATERFALL. IT WAS A MIRACLE!
BUT THE MONSTER WAS WAITING FOR US AT THE BOTTOM.
I WAS SO HAPPY TO SEE THEM, I COULDN'T BREATHE. BUT THE THUNDER OF FOOTSTEPS NEARBY MADE ME FREEZE. EACH FOOTSTEP SENT A COLD SHUDDER DOWN MY BACK.
KOROKO! HE'S COMING!
AND HE'S ALWAYS HUNGRY.
WE HAVE TO GET *OUT!*
THUD
THUD
THUDDDDDD

MAYBE IF WE ALL WORK ON THE CAGE BARS TOGETHER...
WE GRABBED THE WOODEN BARS. THE PRISONERS PUSHED FROM THE INSIDE. WE PULLED FROM THE OUTSIDE.
WE'RE NOT STRONG ENOUGH. THEY WON'T BUDGE. WHAT ARE WE GOING TO DO?

I JUMPED IN SURPRISE AS BENNY LET OUT AN ANGRY GROWL.
YOOOWWWWWWWWRRRR!
RRRRRIPPPPP
SLASSSSSH
BENNY ATTACKED THE BARS LIKE A WILD BEAST. GROWLING AND SPITTING AND SNARLING, HE SHATTERED THE WOOD WITH FRIGHTENING STRENGTH.
THE FOUR PRISONERS RAN OUT. FREE! THEY WERE FREE! BUT THERE WAS NO TIME TO CELEBRATE.

CHAPTER THIRTEEN
BATTLE OF THE MONSTERS
KOROKO!

OVERCOME WITH HORROR, I FROZE AND STARED AT THE HUGE CREATURE. MY LEGS STARTED TO TREMBLE AND I FELT A WAVE OF COLD PANIC WASH OVER ME.
I COULD FEEL HIS HOT BREATH ON MY FACE. THE STENCH--LIKE DEAD ROTTEN FISH--POURED OFF HIS BODY. I STARTED TO CHOKE.
THE MONSTER STARED ANGRILY AT THE SHATTERED CAGE. HE LIFTED IT AS IF IT WERE MADE OF PAPER...
...AND HEAVED IT OVER THE SWAMP.
THEN, GRUNTING AND GROWLING, HIS BIG CHEST HEAVING, THE MONSTER LOWERED HIS GAZE TO US.

I LET OUT A SCREAM AS THE BIG CREATURE MADE A GRAB FOR UNCLE BILL.
NOOOOOOOOOO!
RUN! EVERYONE-- MOVE!
UNCLE BILL DODGED TO THE RIGHT. THE BIG, GRASPING HAND MISSED HIM BY INCHES.
BUT THERE WAS NOWHERE TO RUN. KOROKO HAD US BACKED UP AGAINST THE CAGES.
WE'RE TRAPPED HERE. WE CAN'T FIGHT HIM. WHAT CAN WE DO?
WE ALL SCREAMED AS THE RAGING BEAST CHARGED AT US, BARING ITS JAGGED FANGS, EYES RED WITH FURY.
AAAIIIEEEE!

THE MONSTER GRABBED MR. WOODSON AND RAISED HIM HIGH ABOVE HIS HEAD.
NO! PLEASE!
MR. WOODSON KICKED AND THRASHED HIS ARMS, STRUGGLING TO FREE HIMSELF.
PUT HIM DOWN! PUT MY DAD DOWN! PLEASE--!
AS WE LOOKED ON IN HELPLESS HORROR, KOROKO TOSSED HANNAH'S FATHER TO THE GROUND....
THUD
...AND PICKED ME UP IN HIS PLACE!
NO! PLEASE--! PLEASE--!

THE MONSTER'S CLAWS PINCHED HARD AS HE HELD ME ABOVE HIS HEAD. I SCREAMED AND KICKED, BUT HE HELD ME AS IF I WAS A FEATHER.
THEN HE SLOWLY LOWERED ME...
LOWERED ME TO HIS GAPING MOUTH--AND LICKED MY BACK WITH HIS HOT, FAT TONGUE.
NOOOOOOOOOO!
HE'S GOING TO EAT HER!
HE'S GOING TO EAT US ALL!
SOME-BODY--DO SOMETHING! STOP HIM!

I SHUT MY EYES AS KOROKO DANGLED ME OVER HIS MOUTH. HIS HOT, SOUR BREATH WASHED OVER ME. I HEARD A LOUD GROWL. AND I OPENED MY EYES TO SEE ANOTHER MONSTER ATTACK KOROKO!
WHERE DID THE OTHER MONSTER COME FROM? MY BRAIN SPUN IN CONFUSION. AND THEN SUDDENLY, I REALIZED...
BENNY!!
RRRRROOOOOOAR!
HUUNNNNNNH?

STARTLED BY BENNY'S ATTACK, KOROKO LOOSENED HIS GRIP ON ME, AND I SLID DOWN HIS BODY TO THE GROUND. MY HEART POUNDING, I TURNED AND WATCHED THE TERRIFYING BATTLE.
RRRRRRRRR
GRWWWWWWWLLLL
POWW!
UNNNNHH!
THUD
KOROKO UTTERED A GROAN AS BENNY KNOCKED HIM OFF HIS FEET AND WRESTLED HIM TO THE GROUND.
WOMMP

COULDN'T BREATHE. I COULDN'T MOVE, WATCHING BENNY POUND THE MONSTER WITH PUNCH AFTER PUNCH. BENNY GRUNTED AND GROWLED WITH EACH PUNCH.
QUICK! HELP PULL UP THOSE VINES! WE'LL USE THEM TO TIE THE MONSTER UP!
THESE VINES ARE STRONG. THEY SHOULD HOLD KOROKO IN PLACE.
WHOOOOOAAAAAH!
BUT THE BATTLE WASN'T OVER. WITH A POWERFUL HEAVE, KOROKO THREW BENNY OFF HIM...

WE STARED IN SHOCK AS KOROKO GROANED AND HOBBLED AWAY. LIMPING, HE TRUDGED AWAY, HEAD LOWERED IN DEFEAT.
HUH??
HE'S HAD ENOUGH. HE'S GOING AWAY! BENNY--YOU BEAT HIM!
I DON'T BELIEVE IT!

CHAPTER FOURTEEN
WELCOME TO BEAST ISLAND
HANNAH AND MARCUS AND THEIR PARENTS, UNCLE BILL, DR. NEWTON AND I DANCED AND CHEERED AND SLAPPED HIGH-FIVES AND WENT CRAZY, CELEBRATING THE VICTORY OVER THE MONSTER.
I NOTICED THAT BENNY STOOD GLUMLY ON THE SIDE, WATCHING US. HE DIDN'T JOIN IN.
BENNY-- WHAT'S WRONG?
WHAT'S WRONG? YOU'RE ASKING ME WHAT'S WRONG? I'M A MONSTER, KARLA. LOOK AT ME. I'M A HIDEOUS, GROSS MONSTER!

UNCLE BILL HURRIED OVER TO COMFORT BENNY.
DON'T GIVE UP HOPE, BENNY. AS SOON AS WE GET HOME, I'LL TAKE YOU TO THE SCIENCE LAB. ONE OF MY PARTNERS THERE WILL KNOW--
HOW TO TURN A MONSTER BACK INTO A BOY? I DON'T THINK SO!
IT CAME FROM THE SNAKE VENOM. SO IT'S A CHEMICAL THING. IT CAN BE REVERSED. I'M SURE--
UNCLE BILL DIDN'T GET TO FINISH HIS SENTENCE. HE WAS INTERRUPTED BY...
RIIING
RIIING
RIIING
IT CAME FROM MY BACKPACK! MY PHONE!

HELLO? MOM??
THEY LIED TO US! THEY SAID PHONES DON'T WORK HERE! IT WAS A LIE!
WE WERE SO STUPID! WHY DIDN'T WE TEST OUR PHONES? WHY DID WE JUST BELIEVE THEM?
WE WERE TOO BUSY WITH ALL OUR OTHER PROBLEMS.
HI, MOM. YES, I'M OKAY. UH...WHAT'S THAT? HOW IS THE TRIP GOING?
WELL... IT...UH...IT'S BEEN VERY EXCITING!
WANT TO TALK TO BENNY? I'LL PUT HIM ON...

I'VE... UH...GROWN A LOT.
WE'RE WRAPPING THINGS UP HERE, SIS. WE'LL BE SAILING FOR HOME VERY SOON.
YES, THE KIDS HAVE HAD SOME ADVENTURES TO TELL THEIR FRIENDS ABOUT. WELL...I HAVE TO CONFESS, WE'RE NOT REALLY AT DISNEY WORLD. WE CAN TALK WHEN WE GET BACK.
BUT, YOU KNOW WHAT, SIS? I THINK I'M COMING HOME WITH A ***MILLION DOLLAR*** IDEA! I THINK I'M GOING TO BE FAMOUS AFTER ALL!

UNCLE BILL CALLED FOR HELP, AND A BIG CABIN CRUISER ARRIVED TO TAKE ALL EIGHT OF US OFF THE ISLAND.
UNCLE BILL, WHAT'S YOUR MILLION DOLLAR IDEA?
TELL YOU LATER.
WE KNEW THEY WOULDN'T ALLOW MY MONSTER BROTHER ON AN AIRPLANE, SO WE TOOK A STEAMER ALL THE WAY TO NEW YORK.
WE SAID GOODBYE TO THE WOODSONS AND RENTED A CAR FOR THE DRIVE TO OUR HOME IN CLEVELAND.
MOM IS GOING TO BE VERY UPSET WHEN SHE SEES ME.
NO WORRIES. I'LL HANDLE IT.

WHEN WE ARRIVED HOME...
BILL-- WHAT HAVE YOU DONE TO MY SON??! BILL-- WHAT HAVE YOU DONE?!?
HE HAD A BAD REACTION TO A SNAKEBITE.
A BAD REACTION?! HE'S A MONSTER! MY LITTLE BOY IS A MONSTER!!
I'M SURE THE SCIENTISTS AT MY LAB CAN FIX HIM UP, SIS. BUT I HAVE AN AWESOME IDEA. WE'RE ALL GOING TO BE RICH--AND FAMOUS. YOU'LL SEE!
RICH? FAMOUS? WHAT ARE YOU TALKING ABOUT? ARE YOU CRAZY? LOOK AT HIM! JUST LOOK AT HIM!
I AM LOOKING!

ONE MONTH LATER.
OPENING NIGHT, AND MY NEW MONSTER SHOW IS ALREADY A SENSATION. DRAWING THOUSANDS OF PEOPLE. I *KNEW* IT WOULD WORK!
Welcome to BEAST ISLAND
EVERYONE WANTS TO SEE A REAL MONSTER! GET OUT THERE, BENNY. GO MAKE YOUR FANS HAPPY! ACT LIKE A MONSTER!
I DON'T LIKE THIS, UNCLE BILL. ALL THOSE PEOPLE STARING AT ME...
WE'LL CURE YOU SOON, BENNY. MEANWHILE, PEOPLE ARE PAYING TWO HUNDRED DOLLARS A TICKET! OUR PICTURES ARE IN EVERY MAGAZINE AND NEWS-PAPER ALL OVER THE WORLD!
THE *BEAST ISLAND* THEATER IS TOTALLY FULL! WE'RE SOLD OUT FOR EVERY SHOW!

OOOOOOH LOOOOOK!
WOWWWWWWW!
GIVE THEM A GOOD SHOW, BENNY. JUST THINK--YOU GOT YOUR WISH! YOU'RE A **STAR!!**
THE END

# JUST

# BEYOND™

# ABOUT THE AUTHORS

## R.L. Stine

R.L. Stine is one of the best-selling children's authors in history. His *Goosebumps* and *Fear Street* series have sold more than 400 million copies around the world and have been translated into 32 languages. He has had several TV series based on his work, and two feature films, *Goosebumps* (2015) and *Goosebumps 2: Haunted Halloween* (2018) starring Jack Black as R.L. Stine. *Just Beyond* is Stine's first-ever series of original graphic novels. He lives in New York City with his wife Jane, an editor and publisher.

## Kelly & Nicole Matthews

Kelly and Nichole Matthews are twin sisters (and totally not four cats in a trench coat) who work as freelance comic book artists and illustrators just north of the Emerald City. They've worked on a number of titles that you may have heard of (and maybe even read!) including *Jim Henson's The Power of the Dark Crystal*, *Pandora's Legacy*, and *Toil & Trouble*. They have an original webcomic, *Maskless*, that you can read for free on Hiveworks.

New York Times Bestselling Author

R.L. STINE

# JUST BEYOND

KELLY & NICHOLE MATTHEWS

SCARE SCHOOL

THE SCARE SCHOOL

# YOUR SCARY SNEAK PEEK!

Written by
**R.L. Stine**

Illustrated by
**Kelly & Nichole Matthews**

Lettered by
**Mike Fiorentino**

Cover by
**Julian Totino Tedesco**

# CHAPTER ONE
# THEY SENT A DROGG

EVERY SHADOW MADE ME JUMP. EVERY SOUND SENT A CHILL TO THE BACK OF MY NECK.
I LET OUT A CRY AS DRAKE GRABBED MY ARM AND PULLED ME BACK.
LEEDA-- SOMEONE'S COMING!
I FROZE AND LISTENED. THE HOLLOW THUD OF FOOTSTEPS. APPROACHING. SOMEONE WAS WHISTLING A TUNE.
BUDDY MADE A GULPING SOUND. HE BACKED INTO AN OPEN LOCKER TO HIDE.

MARTY, WHERE'D YOU LEARN TO WHISTLE LIKE THAT?
I'M SELF-TAUGHT.
YOU SHOULD GO ON THAT *AMERICA'S GOT TALENT* TV SHOW.
YOU COULD WIN.
Grease
TRYOUTS!
NAH. WHEN I WHISTLE IN FRONT OF PEOPLE, MY LIPS GET DRY.
The amazing Amaz-O
THEY PASSED BY WITHOUT SEEING US. I REALIZED I WAS HOLDING MY BREATH.
WHEW!
CLOSE ONE.

MAYBE WE SHOULD GO BACK. BEFORE THEY DISCOVER WE ARE GONE.
GO BACK? ARE YOU SERIOUS?
BUDDY, YOU BEGGED US TO COME ALONG. NOW YOU'RE A COWARD?
I'M NOT A COWARD. I'M JUST SCARED.
WE'RE *NEVER* GOING BACK.
C'MON, GUYS--LET'S MOVE.

WE TURNED A CORNER. THE HALL SEEMED ENDLESS.
WE'RE FOLLOWING YOU, LEEDA. CUZ YOU'RE THE *LEEDA!*
HAHA. GET IT?
BUDDY, NO ONE LIKES YOUR JOKES. YOU KNOW THAT, DON'T YOU?
YEAH. I KNOW.
ARE WE WALKING IN CIRCLES? WHERE'S THE EXIT?
AND WHY DO YOU KEEP LOOKING BACK?
MAYBE THEY KNOW WE'RE GONE. MAYBE THEY SENT SOMEONE AFTER US.
TO... TERMINATE US.
KEEP IT UP, BUDDY. KEEP THINKING THOSE GOOD THOUGHTS.

SHUT UP. BOTH OF YOU. SOMEONE'S COMING.
SCORPIONS
WE DUCKED INTO AN EMPTY CLASSROOM.
Don't be jelly sign-up now!
SHE TRIED TO DO A SIMPLE THIGH STAND...AND SHE SPRAINED HER ANKLE.
HAHA. THAT'S SO LAME.
THEY WALKED ON WITHOUT SEEING US.
DID YOU SEE THEIR SCHOOL UNIFORMS?
WEIRD.
WE'RE THE ONES WHO LOOK WEIRD. ANYONE CAN SEE WE DON'T BELONG.
I JUMPED AS BUDDY LET OUT A SCREAM.
I KNEW IT! WE'RE *CAUGHT!*

THEY SENT A DROGG!!

CHAPTER TWO
SAVED BY THE BELL
THE DROGG'S FOUR LEGS KEPT UP A ROBOTIC RHYTHM AS IT BARRELED TOWARD US.
ITS EYES SWUNG MECHANICALLY FROM SIDE TO SIDE.
PROGRAMMED AS A WARRIOR-GUARD WITH THE KILLER INSTINCTS OF A LIVING HUMAN. NO WAY TO FIGHT IT. NO WAY TO ESCAPE IT.
RAISE YOUR HANDS. WE HAVE TO SURRENDER.
NO WAY. I'M NEVER GOING BACK.
THE DROGG BEGAN TO GRUNT AS IT CLOSED IN ON US. IT LOWERED ITS HEAD IN FULL ATTACK MODE.

ITS LEFT EYE IS A CAMERA. THEY'RE WATCHING US!
I SURRENDER! I GIVE UP!
PLEASE DON'T SHOOT!
THEN...A BELL SHATTERED THE SILENCE. A DEAFENING BUZZ THAT RANG DOWN THE LONG HALL AND ECHOED OFF THE TILE WALLS.
VZZZZZZZZ
WHOOOAH!
I GASPED AS CLASSROOM DOORS WERE FLUNG OPEN. KIDS STREAMED INTO THE HALL. LAUGHTER AND LOUD VOICES.

QUICK! LOSE YOURSELF IN THE CROWD. MAYBE WE CAN ESCAPE THE DROGG!
TOO LATE. I SURRENDER! I SURRENDER!
DRAKE GAVE BUDDY A HARD PUSH INTO THE MOB OF KIDS.
I HUNCHED MY SHOULDERS AND DUCKED MY HEAD. I MADE MYSELF AS SMALL AS POSSIBLE. WE KEPT LOW AND FOLLOWED THE STAMPEDE OF KIDS.
I COULDN'T SEE THE DROGG. DID IT GET SWEPT AWAY IN THE CROWD? OR DID IT STILL HAVE ITS LASER EYES TRAINED ON US?

THE KIDS WERE ALL STAMPEDING TO THE AUDITORIUM.
HEY, STOP!
DRAKE, BUDDY, AND I WERE ALMOST TO THE DOOR--WHEN WE WERE SPOTTED...
WHY ARE YOU DRESSED LIKE THAT?
UH... WE'RE IN A BAND.
ARE YOU GOING TO PLAY AT THE ASSEMBLY?
SO THAT'S WHERE THEY WERE ALL GOING. THE WHOLE SCHOOL WAS HEADING TO AN ASSEMBLY.
WHEN THEY'RE ALL INSIDE, WE CAN RUN.
DOES YOUR WHOLE BAND ALWAYS WEAR THOSE SHORT PANTS?
YEAH. WE'RE CALLED *THE SHORTS.*

WE LINGERED BY THE AUDITORIUM AS EVERYONE POURED IN. WE GOT A LOT OF CURIOUS STARES. BUT NO ONE SEEMED SUSPICIOUS.
I KEPT LOOKING FOR THE DROGG, EXPECTING IT TO ROAR BACK AND CLAIM US. BUT SOON, THE HALL WAS EMPTY AND SILENT.
THIS IS OUR CHANCE. LET'S GO!
DRAKE AND I TOOK OFF, OUR SHOES THUDDING IN THE EMPTY HALL. WE DIDN'T GET FAR.
STOP! YOU THREE! STOP RIGHT THERE! WHERE DO YOU THINK YOU'RE GOING?
WELL... UH...
COME WITH ME. RIGHT NOW. YOU'RE NOT GOING ANYWHERE.

CHAPTER THREE
"YOU WILL HAVE TO BE TERMINATED"
TRYING TO DUCK OUT OF THE ASSEMBLY? THAT'S NOT GOING TO HAPPEN.
TAKE THOSE SEATS RIGHT THERE. AND DON'T TRY ANYTHING. I'LL BE WATCHING YOU THE WHOLE TIME.
JUST 'CUZ YOU WORE YOUR HALLOWEEN COSTUMES DOESN'T MAKE YOU SPECIAL.
I BREATHED A SIGH OF RELIEF. HE THOUGHT WE WERE STUDENTS. HE DIDN'T KNOW THE TRUTH.
THAT TEACHER IS STILL WATCHING US.
WE HAVE TO SIT THROUGH THE WHOLE ASSEMBLY.
WE'LL NEVER GET AWAY. I THINK WE SHOULD JUST GO BACK.
DO YOU KNOW YOUR PROBLEM?
YOU'RE YOU!

WE WERE TRAPPED, BUT WE WERE SAFE FOR NOW. THE AUDITORIUM GREW SILENT. ONSTAGE, A MAN STEPPED TO THE PODIUM.
I'M SURE ALMOST ALL OF YOU KNOW ME. I AM GEORGE P. SCARE, YOUR PRINCIPAL AND THE FOUNDER OF THIS SCHOOL.
YES, I NAMED IT AFTER MYSELF. THE SCARE SCHOOL. I WANTED TO START A SCHOOL WHERE NO ONE WOULD BE SCARED TO LEARN OR GROW.
IS THIS GUY FOR REAL? CHECK HIM OUT. DOESN'T HE LOOK A LITTLE LIKE THE MASTER DEAN?
I CAN'T REALLY SEE HIS FACE.
THAT'S TOO CREEPY. EVEN THE MASTER DEAN CAN'T BE IN TWO PLACES AT ONCE...CAN HE?

THIS ISN'T JUST *MY* SCHOOL. IT'S *YOUR* SCHOOL, TOO. THAT'S WHY MY DOOR IS ALWAYS OPEN TO YOU.
THIS IS SO LAME. CAN'T WE GET OUT OF HERE?
THAT TEACHER KEEPS LOOKING OVER HERE.
WE'RE A FAMILY. WE HAVE TO BE ALERT AND PROTECT EACH OTHER.
WE MUST KEEP WATCH FOR INVADERS. WE MUST GUARD OUR HOUSE.
ALL INVADERS MUST BE RECOGNIZED--*AND STOPPED.*
HUH? INVADERS? WHAT IS HE TALKING ABOUT?
ARE *WE* THE INVADERS?
QUICK. THAT TEACHER LEFT. HURRY. LET'S *GO.*

THE DROGG! IT'S BEEN WAITING FOR US!
GO!
SCORPIONS

Jenna Ayoub

# FOREVER HOME™

HOO-
HOO!

HE'S RATHER DENSE, ISN'T HE? WHAT SHALL WE DOOO...?
OH, I DO LOVE THE PIANO TRICK. WHY DON'T WE TRY THAT?
HOO-HOO! OH YES, GLADYS! DO!

HE OUGHT TO HEAR IT FROM DOWN HERE.
THEY BOUGHT SUCH A LOVELY LITTLE UPRIGHT, IT'D BE A SHAME NOT TO TRY IT!

WHAT ARE YOU TWO DOING...?
Nothing!♪

IF YOU PLEASE, MAESTRO.
OH-HOO! YOU'RE TOO KIND!

SERIOUSLY?!
HUSH, DEARIE. AN ARTIST IS AT WORK.

QUIT IT, YOU GUYS! YOU'RE NOT GONNA SCARE MY PARENTS--
WHAT IS THAT DREADFUL SOUND?!

C'MON, KNOCK IT OFF!
H'OOOOH! MY SECOND HUSBAND USED TO PLAY THE PIANO...!
HOOO!
GLADYS!
VIOLA!
WHY ARE YOU LIKE THIS?!

A-PLUS EFFORT, THOMAS!
NO! FENRIR! BE QUIET, YOU!

WILLOW!

STOP MAKING SO MUCH NOISE!
AHOOO!
HOO-HOOOO!!!
REEEEHHHH!!
HOO!

WHA--?!
I--!!
...'KAY, DAD. SORRY.
REH.

IT DIDN'T WORK, VIOLA.
DO YOU SUPPOSE HE COULD TELL THAT I DON'T KNOW HOW TO PLAY THE PIANO?
OH YES, GLADYS. VERY MUCH SO.
WE'LL HAVE TO TRY SOMETHING ELSE..

OoOO-HOOo HOO-HOOOO!
GUYS! QUIT IT!
DAD

DAD

OKS
BOOKS

STOP RIGHT THERE!

YOU TWO ARE OUT OF CONTROL AS OF LATE, AND WILLOW HAS TASKED ME WITH KEEPING ORDER.
HOO-HOO! WHAT AN EXCELLENT JOB YOU'RE DOING, DEAR TOMMY.

OH YES. DEAR, SWEET, TOMMY. SO FULL OF GOOD INTENTIONS.
SO BRAVE.

BUT NO MAN HAS EVER KEPT US FROM WHAT WE WANTED, THOMAS.

LADY...?
A-hoooo

THOMAS?
HOO. HOOoo

THEY WERE LIKE...
WILD ANIMALS ...WILLOW.
YOU DID YOUR BEST, SOLDIER.

Hoo-
Hoo-
Hoo!
CLICK!

WHAT ON EARTH DO YOU THINK *THIS* IS, GLADYS?
I HAVEN'T THE SLIGHTEST IDEA, VIOLA!
DROP IT DOWN THE LAUNDRY CHUTE WITH THE OTHER THINGS, DO! HOO-HOO!
CLICK

QUIT PLAYING WITH THE LIGHTS!
...AND PUT THAT DOWN! THAT'S MY DAD'S!

CLICK!

CLICK

UGGHH!

WHOOF!
'CHOO!

DID YOU FEEL THAT?
NOPE.

THEY'RE GIVING YOU A HARD TIME, AREN'T THEY?
YOU SHOULD PROBABLY JUST GIVE UP.
SAVE YOURSELVES THE TROUBLE.

HOO-HOO! IT'S NO TROUBLE AT ALL, DEARIE!
WE'RE QUITE ENJOYING OURSELVES!

BESIDES! WE'VE NEVER SHIED AWAY FROM A CHALLENGE.
IT ISN'T IN OUR NATURE!